Into the Hedge

Knights of the Autumn Crown

Book one

Marko Tomasz Duraj

This is a work of fiction. Similarities to real people, places, or events are entirely coincidental.

INTO THE HEDGE

First edition. December 15, 2024.

Copyright © 2024 Marko Tomasz Duraj.

ISBN: 979-8230420194

Written by Marko Tomasz Duraj.

"Gdzie diabeł nie może, tam babę pośle."

"Where devil cannot go, he will send a woman."Polish Proverb

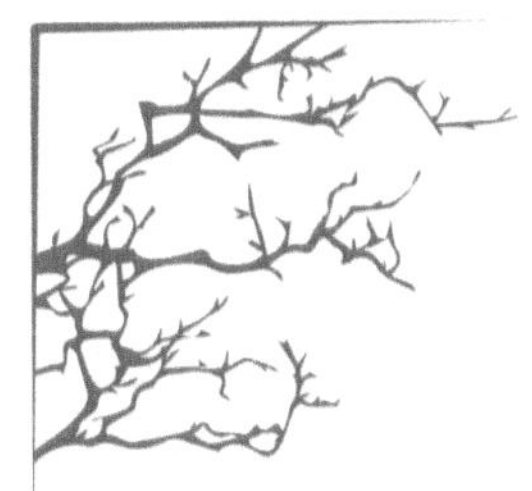

Chapter One

Within a small wooded area. An ominous and titanic crescent moon glides through an early evening. Thick clouds and dense foliage allowed only sparse moonlight to seep through. Noises of nocturnal wildlife serenade the environment.

A young woman, in her late teens, awoke within this murky forest. Her vision slowly comes into focus. Groaning as she stood sucking in the air from the soreness of injury. Grass stains and wet dirt coated various parts of her jeans and jacket. Sharp thorns stung her fingers as she ran them through jet-back curls.

She examined her condition, muttering curses with exasperation. Signs of what led to this event confused her while trying to rationalize the outcome. She had tumbled down, but from where? The area was too dense with twisted trees and blade-like vines. The marks on the ground appeared to come from the barricade of woods. She shook her head. It wasn't possible...

Soft, low whispers emanated from the shadows, with no discernible location but from the shifting shadows themselves.

"Josh? Mandy?" She called out "Anyone here?

Leaves quivered from as branches waved along with the wind. From the corner of her eye, a dark form moved into the tree line, staring at her. The young woman turned to face the stranger,

"Alex...?! Is that you?? It better not be!" An intense glare in her blue eyes. She reached for the first object within reach. Grabbing a stick from the ground, she pitched it at the unflinching figure. Leaves rustled as the stick flew away into the dark.

"Aes!" Strange, ephemeral whispers called out from the dark.

"Who? Who is there?" She asked, turning her head several times to find the source.

"Aes! Come her'eh." They called again. It was stronger. Clearer this time. Save for an odd accent of words that gave it a nasally tone.

"Ch'yea.." She scoffed. Shining her phone's light upon the form, but there was no one there. Her breath quickened as she turned to face each beckoning. Shining her light upon the shadows.

For a quick moment, the moonlight blacked out completely. Something had flown overhead, just low enough to sway the tree and break several branches. An undercurrent whipped her off balance, falling back into the damp grass.

Aes!" The Whispers started again. "Aes! You must hide."

"Who is 'Aes'?"

"You are Aes! My De'ah."

"No, I'm not!"

"Quiet! He will hear you!!"

"Who? Who will hear me??"

Something appeared off in the distance, towering over the woods. An enormous silhouette in the dim light of the night sky. Its titanic revelation was a sinister image worn on her mind. She gasped, her breath catching in her throat. She practically ripped the jeans pocket, pulling free her rosary. Clasping them in her petite hand.

Sets of glowing green lights emerged from what seemed to be the head. Illuminating areas of the land like an alien spotlight as it exhausted several gusts of steam. All sorts of natural debris hung from the thing.

The foliage began to rustle with a light breeze before a forceful gust blew throughout the dense woods, accompanied by an otherworldly mix of dissonant screams, ghostly winds, and a disembodied roar. Foul swampy muck flew into the air as several branches cracked and fell.

"AES, HIDE!" The echoing whispers called out, "FOLLOW MY VOICE! HURR'EY!"

Stricken with the bitter cold of fear, 'Aes' frantically clawed along the ground, trying to rise up and run in the opposite direction. The ungodly spotlights turned in her direction. Focusing upon her clumsy movement, before unleashing some infernal sound that caused the foliage to rustle lightly, a forceful gust blew throughout the dense woods, accompanied by an otherworldly sound, as if it were a mix of dissonant screams, ghostly winds, and a disembodied roar. Shutting her ears in pain from the noise, Aes stumped from its dizzying effect.

The surrounding earth began to rip apart as roots and buried plants were torn from their burls. As the massive thing moved through the woodlands. Sounds of brush and robust thorny vines being ripped from underfoot. Rock, tree, or vine. Nothing could withstand its pure raw force. A sudden thundering of tremors shook the weird grove, several old and rotten logs breaking off to the ground.

Dashing through the uneven terrain. Aes sought refuge within the density of the forest. From one deformed tree to another, she moved. Thunderous sounds reverberated in the night. Piercing the natural canopy, the lights were the only thing that discerned the location of this titan. Closer and closer through the growing walls of twisted woods, it moved. Destruction paved in its wake

"Ov'ah The'ah!" The whispers alerted the girl.

Fate smiled. If only for this one moment of flickering hope, she spotted a rotted out tree. It lay on its side and might have been large enough to hide. She would have to time it just right to evade the shifting search lights as they aimed closer to her position. From under the cover of the heavy brush, the lights swung past the hiding spot.

Rising up, her unadjusted eyes lead her into a web of vines. Gripping her jacket, jeans, and tangling hair. The movement captured the attention of the seeker and traced the illuminated focus backwards to that point. Aes froze in place as the light lingered a painful moment before moving on. She took the chance.

She powered through webs of sharp hooks. Rending the fabric from her skin and breaking clumps of hair. Tiny streams of red ran down from open wounds. Aes ran as fast and as hard as she could. The pounding drum of her heartbeat in her ears. Panting hard with every demanding action. Trying desperately to move past both stationary and moving obstacles. She dodged, jumped, and dove through the dark forest, adrenaline pushing her forward.

The heavy sounds of this thing's movement thundered and echoed in the night. Tremors cracked the land. She dared not look back. Even so, the danger grew. She dashed under the hollowed tree. Though it was dark, glimmers of moonlight poured through the holes of the cracked bark as well as opening on the other side. Aes squatted down in the tiny alcove, red beads rolling between her fingers as she quietly whispered prayers. She could feel the steady shaking of the ground and the falling debris from within her haven.

Looking up, her eyes widened with fear. Several feet directly overhead, the sight of the huge jaws All sorts of natural debris hung down from or could have been a part of this thing. Sounding like the exhaust of a heavy machine, gusts of steam kicked up dust and debris, as if sniffing something, creating a humid condition. Aes went pale as a ghost. Strains of oozing slime dangled from protruding uneven teeth. She places both hands over her mouth while remaining still. Despite the goop landing on her arm.

"Aes, jump!" The whispers spoke again. The young woman glanced down. Several yards from her was an overlook. To what and were, wasn't visibly discernible. The blinding pale green lights flourished once more. The illuminated beams inches away, Aes pulled her knees in tight.

A large chuck of rotten wood fell close by. The entire dead tree crumbled and rocked as the thing leaped from the top. The force of its weight shook the ground under her feet. It invoked horror in her eyes, watching as the ground gradually collapsed. Aes tried to find something, anything, to grab as she was sent tumbling down the decaying slope.

A heavy splash of stagnant swamp water flew into the air as Aes implemented within. The murky mud sucked in her feet and lower back. Holding her head with dazed motion, she struggled to sit up. Air sucked down the silt as she muscled herself free, trying to stand. Each step sank into the dark swamp, seeing no other means of moving onwards. She was visibly uncomfortable, but with gritted teeth, continued to push forward.

A large shadow blocked the light of a hauntingly giant moon. Aes looked back to see the giant monster, leaves, thorns, and vines still tangled up around its body. Sniffing the air in search of her. Its silhouette over the moon gave it a more terrifying image than before.

"This way..." the whispers started again. More discernible this time.

"Come this way, de'ah." Aes looked forward and whispered back.

"Who is there, who are you?" But there was no answer to her question, just a repeat of the instructions.

"Come this way, my de'ah Aes."

She moved through the shadowy water, damp and cold. The murky water lapped at her waist and chest, the wet fabric clinging to her curves as slime and algae stuck to her skin.

"Who are you?!" She demanded in a hushed tone.

"I can help you, de'ah, girl." The whispers replied

The thundering steps of the stalking beast came down to the swampy land. Its industrial breath coated the air as it sniffed. Leaping with great power, the thing landed its great weight on several large trees, their roots exposed over the marsh and mud. Slight cracking sounds from the trees as they adjusted for the creature's weight.

Aes watched the beast from hidden under the roots of a tree. It was just low enough that she could squad under it. The beast's eyes were like spot lights, beaming down on the marsh beneath itself. Pulling herself deeper under the tree, swampy marsh water rose to her thighs as she squatted down to hide. She watched as it searched the area with its burning gaze.

"Come Aes! Come this way, my de'ah." The whispers had more clarity of direction now. She didn't like the idea of leaving the spot. Aes stayed as low and as quiet as possible. Looking up every other step, she watched the thing from below.

It leapt again, changing vantage points in an effort to spot the night's prey. Aes took the opportunity to move quicker in the voice's direction.

"Up he'ah, up he'ah!" The voice called from an elevated position of its own. A natural arch way within one of the trees, just large enough for her to enter. She climbed up the roots and looked inside.

Suspended from a weatherworn rope. A bent frame of a metal lantern gently rocked back and forth.

"Hello, my de'ah, Aes." The lantern spoke, a slight radiant pulse as it spoke with a conniving, high-pitched tone of a greasy trickster. An outline of a wide, grinning face. A predominately pointed chin and beak-like nose. It's hollow, beady yellow eyes stared directly at her from within. The lantern's glow revealed her features with more clarity. She had a soft, delicate beauty, slightly decorated with freckles. Wide, upturned blue eyes, full lips, and a button nose in the center of expressive features. Thick black curls cascaded past her shoulders.

"Who..WHAT..are you?" She demanded.

"I can help ya, Aes," the object answered.

"Why do you keep calling me that?"

"That is ya name, my de'ah childe."

"No, it is not!"

"It is! Git in, he'ah," it said more firmly.

"How are... 'you' supposed to help me?" Aes demanded. Seeking shelter within the willow's cavity.

"All ya gotta do is let me out!" The lantern answered with an eerie grin. Aes squinted in suspicion at the diabolical features she could discern.

"I dunno..." She answered.

"The'ah, ain't much time! I think the Cu has your scent again! Hurr'ey!"

Aes gestured with the sign of the cross. Touching her head and shoulders before inspecting the metal work. The glow within allowed just enough light to study this little prison.

"It's too weird... I can't figure it out." She informed the glowing face.

A booming voice broke the quiet from behind her. The thing had returned. Aes snapped back just in time to see the blazing infernal stare of a great beast. Two sets of eyes on its head blinded her with such intensity. She turned away just as the beast's maw seized her by the ankle. Tearing the young woman from the knotted archway. She screamed in horror. Holding the lantern hopelessly to secure her. The rotted rope snapped with ease as she was carried out. Reflexively, Aes swung the lantern viciously at the mouth. The thick matted foliage on the thing absorbed the blows.

"Rise the lantern!" The spirit within ordered

"What?" Aes shouted

"DO IT!"

Aes did so. The light inside grew brighter until it released a blinding flash. The thing jumped back, releasing the human to fall, making a large splash into the swampy water below. Ripples in the air, from the effect, slowly dissipated. Kicking and flailing. Aes waded through the marsh as hard and as fast as possible, desperate to get out of the water fast. Fighting and forcing her legs to move as the swamp seemed to suck each foot in until she could make it to a spot of solid ground. The light from the lamp led her.

Her left foot sank deeply into the mud, freezing the fragile mortal in place. She looked back only for a moment before the spirit spoke again.

"Don't be look'n at it!"

Regaining its sense, the giant beast looked directly at her again. It snarled several times. Clawing the ground like a bull with lion-like paws, about to charge. The wild plant growth from its face was like barbed wire, with its thick thorns.

"I'M STUCK!" She cried out, attempting to pry her foot loose.

The whispering voice muttered some odd words to her. Followed by "Say it!" Confused, but with no time to debate, Aes shouted the strange phrase.

The giant beast rammed her, snapping and biting. Aes shrieked as a massive thorn plunged deep into her left shoulder, breaking off from the vine it sprouted from. Dire moments before a burst of black smoke sucked the human inside.

The beast emerged through the black wisps. Its truck-sized head slammed into a dying tree, shattering rotten wood into splinters. blindly crushing the hollow tree with its massive jaws. Aes was nowhere to be seen.

"Good, good..." The whispering voice cackled.

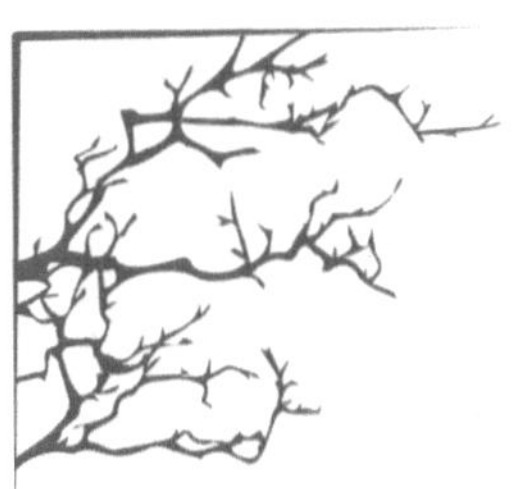

Chapter Two

Dark smoke soared unrestrained through the air. Creeping through the brush and barbs, neither the broadest trunk nor the sharpest thorn could stop it. As small as a tiny bat, the smog gained volume until it was large enough to push Aes, from within, to the ground. She rolled through the brush upon hitting the floor.

Her teeth chattered quickly behind blue lips as she shivered.

"W'hat h..happ'end?"

"No time, keep qui't!" The Spirit replied.

Aes snapped her head back to the roar of the giant thing. Light from its burning eyes pierced through the crevices of the dark forest, creating dozens of tiny hellish beams. Looking in several directions for a path to escape, she hesitated, second-guessing which way to run. If she could get away in time.

" Th'air hide!" The lantern instructed. Rocking towards a tiny opening under a tree. Aes opened her mouth as if to speak. Dashed towards the potential source of shelter. Out of her peripheral vision, streams of light came closer to informing the thing of the human's location.

They grazed the surface of her jacket, transforming to a stream of harsh, burning, green flame. An immense force, focusing solely on that point. A harsh, infernal word hummed in the air as the thing spoke in the unknown language again. Bulldozing everything within its path. Aes scarcely slipped within the hole, mere moments before the timbers came crashing down upon her.

The thing reigned down the full force of its might. Massive jaws tossing foliage and debris, its four eyes scorched the land with the intensity of its focused glare. Deathly howls shattered the surroundings. Rocks smashed, trees splintered, vines torn up from the roots. It scarred the area from the lingering flames.

Just under the onslaught of the environment. Aes was curled up within a ball. Partly buried among the roots and wet ground. Shielding her ears from the noise. The enchanted lantern crammed painfully in her ribs. The ground quaked for what felt like an eternity.

”Don't move, don't look it in the eye!”

The spirit within the lantern warned. But several times, she peeked from her hiding place. What was this thing? She has only seen glimpses of it. Mere pieces of a large puzzle her mind had to fill.

“Do.. NOT!” the spirit barked, catching Aes squinting through the spaces in the roots to see what was happening. She dove down just as the glowing light flashed in her direction. Once more, however, she tried to investigate. Once more, the spirit scolded her. “Ya got a vice of curiosity...”

The flow of this eternity, which lasted over ten minutes, took its toll on the wary human. Her eyelids became heavier. Drained adrenaline demanded its payment. Even as the carnage continued, Aes gradually lost consciousness from exhaustion.

Whatever this creature, this thing was, that scourged the land. The moon'sradiance struggled to break through. From the uprooted dense brush and warped trees. To thick gray fog. It filled with an unnatural stillness. No wind or animal made a sound that could be heard, if anything has survived.

Under the roots of the tree, within the hole, Aes took shelter in. Swamp water gradually filled it up to the tip of her chin. Her dark hairs drifted over the surface. Shifting in her sleep caused her to slip lower within, waking violently into a fit of gasping coughs after inhaling the rank fluids into her nose.

Aes stood up, or tried to, only to be forced back down from the collapsed tree she hid under. Slipping back into the small pond, another choking gasp entered her lungs. Emerging to the surface, Aes frantically battled the environment.

Muscles tightened up around her chest. Brutally expunging phlegm in short, impulsive wheezing for air. Aes pulled open her jacket with one hand, tugging at her shirt collar with the other. Neck and shoulders tensing hard with each cough as she tilted her head back for air. Snaking her hand into any opening she could find with a touch, no form of escape was apparent. Darkness shrouded any sense of direction. Untold amounts of tree and rubble had buried her...alive.

Thunderous pounding in her chest flooded her body. Clawing, grasping at anything to dig or remove. She needed to make an escape. Distressed whimpering took over her coughing fit. Aes began to plead and pray frantically for intervention through tears of fearful sobbing.

Bubbles floated up from underneath. A vacuum caught her foot down in the mud. Hopelessly kicking and pulling to free herself. Tips of her fingernails chipped while trying to grab roots. Letting out a horrid scream while being drug down into the sinking mud. Muck and water covered her head, bubbles of air floating up from where she had been.

She plummeted down through a long, dank hole, still kicking and waving her arms. Letting out a slight grunt that echoed as it drugged her off with the rolling muck, deep into a burrow. She landed knee-deep in mud. Swamp water drenched over her from above.

A muffled sound had been growing from the darkness. Calm and low, it had repeated over and over until...

" AES!!!!!" The spirit inside the lantern broke through her panic attack. "Focus Childe, focus!"

It had fallen a few feet from her, halfway buried in mud. Aes took the source into her arms, clasping it for comfort. Its strange warmth grounded her from the overwhelming fear.

"I'm trapped, I..."

"Childe! You need ta FOCUS! KYRRE!"

"Khr-ee??"

The lantern shifted in hue in response to the word. A low soft blue glow, releasing a gentle stream that fluttered towards her face, soaking into her eye, which began to glow. Aes stared upon the light with a near vacant expression. The glow in her eyes soothed her fears. Physical and mental strain was visually released from her body. Gradually, Aes became docile and clam.

"Good, good." The Spirit said, in a familiar chucking tone.

The entranced state gradually faded. Breathing slowly and deeply as the radiant glow dimed in her eyes. The young human became self-aware once again. A slight shake of her head, blinking and yawning, the questions became apparent on her face.

"What happened?" she muttered to no one specifically.

Faint particles drifted through the air. Gradually illuminating the area with a dull blueish green, Florissant glow. Aes looked around, puzzled. Several forms of fungi and mushrooms slowly lit up from the noise that echoed throughout. The spirit was silent for the time.

Noticing a web of roots and branches, Aes reached out to grab them, hoping to herself free. Low grunts echoed throughout the cavern. As she pulled hard, more of the dark muck gradually bled upon her from overhead. Slime on her palms made her hands slip out. Getting a better grip, she gritted her teeth, trying harder. A hollow gulp released her from the sinkhole. Her enchanted companion still half sunk behind her.

Groaning with frustration, she wiped her face. "At least I can see." She looked back up at the area where she fell, though. "Not getting back up that way." She sighed.

Turning back at the glowing fungus, she gave it several gentle pokes with the tip of the leather shoe. They seemed harmless enough and provided more ambient light. She searched for something that could be used to get the lantern out without herself being stuck again. There were several roots and branches all around. Many were still full of life. A few allowed her to break off into a stick. "This should do it."

She stretched her improvised tool towards the lamp. Tapping it several times, struggling to claw it out. Each noise from her attempt released a metallic echo that shifted the color of the fungus. A slight twitch each time.

"Almost..." she gruffs after each failure.

Aes was completely unaware of the distant, padded sounds began to resonate from beyond. Odd muttering that sounded like open chewing. From out of the darkness, a small bluish creature emerged. It was scraggly, thin, with a pointed stick. A wide pumpkin head that twisted around. Its wide mouth and jagged teeth made nauseating noises as it muttered. Its padded feet squished the wet soil underneath. It seemed to not even notice the human at all. Something else caught its attention...

The eerie glow of the fungus reflected off the buttons of her jeans and jacket. The subterranean creature noticed this. With a joyful sound, it reached out for one of the metallic buttons mindlessly.

"Almost..got.."

"Aes, hurr'ey. Somethin' comin' is wa'ey"

"GOT IT!" Aes said victoriously after she managed to hook the handle with the stick. Struggling to pull it from the mud.

Her expression changed suddenly as she felt something pulling at her jeans. She snapped her head back to see the freakish dwarf trying to claw at her backside. Her iris' shrank into small dots at the sight of this thing and whatever it was trying to do. Reflexively, she turned around with the full force of the stick. The tiny being fell back, having just torn the button free. Aes barely made contact, flinching to her shoulder injury. The tiny being took a single look at her and squeezed and scrambled away, making loud, strange sounds that echoed throughout the caves.

"Ya done, did it now."

"Did what?!"

"At was a'mite', 'ey don't go alone. 'Bout a dozen of em, at least. Need ta git out, fast!"

Aes returned to fishing out the lamp. She raked at it vigorously until it came loose. Upon success, she took the opportunity to rush back to the hole she fell through, trying to climb her way back up. There was no way back. She kept slipping and sliding back to the bottom. Mud and muck were stuck over her body and clothes. The glow of the cavern lit up with the noises of the small creature. It had returned with several others. Each making rapid muttering sounds.

"Don't move!" The Spirit said, "Ther'eh near'ley blind, but hear well!"

Aes froze in place. Her face paled with fear as the strange creatures came towards her. Their heads jerked and snapped in several directions. Inspecting the area.

Aes sat and stared intensely as one waddled closer in her direction. A pointed stick in its hands. It grabbed the glowing spore and took bites out of it. She made no movement and made no sound. The creature squatted down, continuing its meal. Though it never seemed to look directly at her.

She gasped quietly as the mites stabbed the glowing fungi with their makeshift spears. Making the most nauseating sounds as they smacked with open jaws. Aes looked around the area for a potential escape, holding her breath as she did so. Though she found herself sunk too deep into the soaked soil to make one.

This mite paid her no mind, not even noticing her hesitance. One misstep, however, caused her to slip back and fall into the muck. The creature looked in her direction with a bizarre shriek.

Another moved in. Aes pushed herself against the edge of the mud as it got closer, poking its stick around in investigation. It jabbed her in the ribs, and she let out a scream more of fear than pain. Each of the small blue beings looked in her direction, releasing their own sounds of distress. All three turned to run in fear, abandoning their food and weapons.

Aes blinked several times.

"Yeah, okay..." she said, a bit confused.

Reaching out to a gnarled root again, she freed herself much easier this time. Moist, slimy muck covered her clothes. She shook herself to remove what she could from her body.

"Any idea how to get out of here?" She asked, looking around for the lantern.

"Back up, search for a source a wat'ah, and follow it."

"At least I got an answer." she grumbled.

Aes watched the cavern for the chattering creatures. She picked up one of the wooden spears left behind. Lifting the lantern to illuminate her way, she took in the surroundings. Getting a better sense of direction. Phosphorescent fungus stretched throughout the cavern. She took deliberate and light steps forward into the cave.

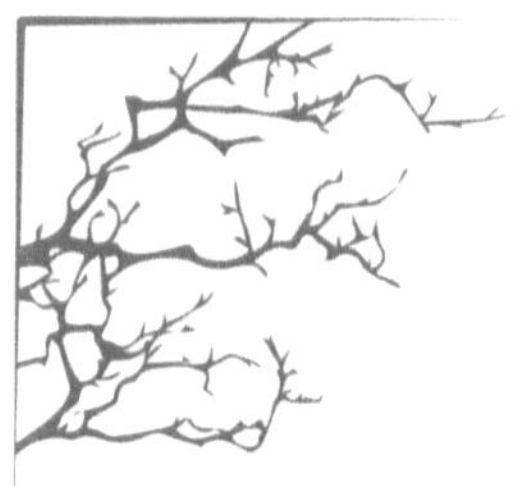

Chapter Three

"Who are you, by the way?" Aes asked.

"Tell you lat'eh de'ah," the Spirit replied.

The human rolled her eyes at the response. Muttering something under her breath, she pushed forward into the cave. All around, high-pitched humming of the fungus played a disharmonious tune. Each twitching in response to some strange and unknown stimulation. They had grown up alone, the walls into a large arch, taking the formation of a great maw. A very unwelcoming sight, Aes took in a deep breath before continuing on.

Each step released a murky liquid from the ground. Aes kept her body knelt as she moved. A sudden, flat knock echoed from under her. She stopped suddenly. Looking directly at her right foot. She was standing over a worn yet worked tile. Using the light from the lantern. She leaned down, looking at the flooring. Slowly bringing the light forward to follow the tiles.

As her eyes adjusted to the ambient glow. A tall form came into view. Aes froze, eyes wide, as she looked up at it in motionless form. An appendage, an arm most likely, extended up and forward as if pointing or waving.

"What is this? A statue?" she asked.

"Move me closer." The spirit replied

Slowly rising from the light for a better view, Aes noticed the form stood upon a chiseled stone block, covered in thick, damp moss. Raising the light farther, she looked upon a weathered stone statue. Its form cracked and decayed. Missing half of its arm and face. Someone placed several random objects at the base of the carved stone. Rocks, strange bones, ripped-up fungus, and sharpened sticks.

"Childe! You need to leave, he're. fast!" The spirit commanded.

"What is it?" Aes responded.

Echoes of chittering bounced off the walls. Aes looked back at the entrance. An unknown number of silhouettes moved into the line of sight between her and the ambient light. Their dull gray eyes seemed to glow in reflection of the shift in radiance. Changing her posture to a more aggressive stance with the sharpened sticks, she braced for a potential attack.

The 'mites' began moving in. Aes watched as their hideous eyes got closer to her. Pulling the sleeve of her jacket down over her hand, she made a second attempt at the makeshift spear. She shrieked upon tightening her hand. Seizing her arm in pain from the hooked barb. The subterranean creatures responded to her shriek with louder, more aggressive noises. They begin to swarm with surprising intellect. Several of them are moving in circular directions and to higher elevations. Aes dropped the light, grabbing the wooden spear with her right hand as she turned to face the attackers.

It was nearly impossible to see in the dim light. The echoes of chittering mites made their location difficult to decipher. Aes shifted her body, aiming the wooden spear at any sign of movement. Even alternations in radiance and color of the glowing mushrooms caused her to twitch.

Two sets of large bullfrog eyes advancing towards her from out of the darkness. They were merely a yard away before Aes spotted their dull gray shine reflecting the changing colors in the room. She rose from the stick and yelled out "Get back!" in a horse tone.

This did nothing to slow the creatures moving towards her. Their misshapen heads gave them a slight zombie-like waddle. A foul smell, like rotten fish, swarmed from the creases of their limbs. Making a mushy noise while clicking their tounges, like some form of echolocation.

A face full of disgust, Aes arched her back to swing viciously at one of them... and missed. The slime from the spear slipped its way from her grasp, disappearing into the darkness. Overzealous momentum spun Aes off balance. Forcing her down on her knees to the slick tile floor. The bulbus little dwarves turned their heads to the side, the way a bird would.

Close enough to see the minute details in the dim light. Aes recoiled at their revealed puffy faces. Pale blue with large swollen heads. Flapping fish jaws with rows of tiny pointed teeth and dopy ears. Wearing rags and bare clawed feet. From overhead, one leaped down from a rock. Its weight brought down upon her back. Aes slammed into the ground, breath expelled from her lungs. The dwarfish assailants swarmed the young human during the altercation.

They pulled at her hair, clothes, and anything else on her person. Aes kicked and punched blindly, gasping for breath. Several of the creatures yelped, ceasing their mugging in retreat. Though not without random objects from her person. The others were not so easily deterred and continued the attack. They tore at her jacket and jeans. Tearing off buttons, zippers, and other metallic, shining objects. Victorious, these mites fled. Yipping louder and quicker as she ran off. Leaping or dancing with webbed palms rose high is a display of the metal pieces.

Aes continued her flailing against any perceived enemy. Settling down once, no opponent was consciously visible. Panting and juddering, she pawed at her hair and torn clothes, with tears flowing from her face. Seizing a stick, left behind by another of the mites. She aimed it outwardly. Backing towards her lantern, she prepared for another attack. Chest rising and falling, heavy.

"Keep the lantern within ya hand. Is the only way I can help!" The Spirit told her. A moment passed before Aes nodded in response. Her breath calmed slowly.

Unaware of the small hand creeping up. Aes was far too focused outwardly. One of the remaining mites reached out for the glittering rosary. Dangling hypnotically on her left wrist. Its silvery surface gleamed like a diamond in the eyes of this petty thief. Slowly, it reached out to the reflective shimmer of the Crucifix. Both bulging bullfrog eyes locked on to the treasure.

Its clawed hand slowly clenched the icon. A sickening hiss of acidic burbling emanated from its tightened grip. Aes shrieked again as the deformed dwarf released a high-pitched roar from the shadows beside her. Unaware of the thick club that shot out from the darkness, striking her hard in the temple. Aes slumped back, her eyes rolled back, as her head rocked back and forth. Her grumbling assailant emerged from the dark. Whining at the seared cross mark on its palm.

Aes lay unconscious, a dark purple swelling on the outside of her left eye. Head rocking back and forth, slowly regaining consciousness. Forceful, inaudible whispers from the spirit called out to her.

"Aes...!"

The human only grunted in response.

"...My De'ah. Awaken!"

With blurry vision, Aes rolled over. Pawing at the lantern like an annoying alarm clock, back arching, knees pulled in to prop herself up. A glazed expression met with the spirit's own otherworldly face.

"You are not without peril yet, childe, now rise!"

With small breathy gusts of exhaustion. Aes reached out to lift the lantern. A sudden sucking of air as she flinched. Grabbing her shoulder in pain. Blood had begun leaking from the thorn in her shoulder. She rocked forward into a kneeling potion, the top of her head resting upon the statue's base. Her hair rolled from side to side as she shook her head.

"You must!" It said with more command.

It took several increasingly deeper inhales before Aes lifted herself upright. A bloody palm of her right hand pressed against the base to push herself up. One foot, then the other. Aes now stood on her feet. Enchanted lamp on her left. Whimpering sounds escaped her. The soreness of the strike to her head snapped her drive in place of a small headache.

A black ink bubbled from under the bloody handprint. Producing tiny needle-like quills that pierced the petite red mark, sucking the blood into the very stones. The face of the ruined statue shifted in distorting expression. It's static head turning to look directly at the young human.

A shadowy figure oozed upon the walls from behind the stone carving, though Aes didn't notice. It bled along the cave rock seamlessly. At first, mimicking the figure. The silhouette tugged violently on each of its own limbs, as if to rend them free from some unseen shackle. It grew more and more distorted, unnatural, and inhuman. Each appendage, legs, arms, neck, and head stretched out to disproportional length. It's the most disturbing of all. Its shadow puppet-like face. A bird-like nose, blunted large teeth that sat inside a hung gaping jaw. near obscure vacant pits for eye sockets.

It stalked after the unaware human, shambling forward with a jerky motion. Riding along the surface of the wall. The shadow was so large, it arced from one side of the cave down to the other. Legs lumbering on the right, while misshapen head suspended from the left. Its sense of location caused the head to twist the serpent-like neck around to be upright. A twisted grin appeared on the wall where it appeared. An insidious hissing voice echoed from the corners, murmuring strange and unsettling words. Only one was audibly comprehendible.

"... LIIIFE!"

Aes stopped for a moment. Minor bumps on her arms and neck peaked. Lantern held high. She turned around to confront the source of this sensation, but there was nothing.

"I can.." She began

"I hear it too. Be on your guard!" The Lantern replied.

Nervously, she took two steps back before resuming her way within the caverns, cautious of the dwarfish mites that dwelled within. With tired legs and sore feet, her unplanned exposition continued. A soft gurgle in the pit of her stomach, Aes leaned forward slightly. Resting her left arm across her abdomen. All around, the luminous mushrooms twitched and hummed. Their color fading into darker, redder versions of blue.

Up ahead, the dwarfish mites froze in fear. Floppy ears flicked and twisted. One after another, the small beings screeched in fear as they sought refuge. Abandoning their trinkets and treasures for safety. Some seeking sanctuary far away within the cave, others watched, trembling from the cracks and crevasses. The ambient light from the lantern followed by a darker presence.

Enormous frog eyes watched the shade stretch its inhuman limbs towards the unaware human. Though nothing was visible to the human eye. The dark form stretched out its black silhouette limb towards the small creatures. Retrieving from a small archway from where they hid a small curved knife. The blade hovered in the air towards the human.

The cave radiated an ungodly deep red from the twitching fungus. Still humming a dissonant tone, but now is a lower octave. Aes, still slightly dazed, faced nearly a dozen mites who had emerged with clubs and spears drawn. They hopped and stamped their feet. Snarled with gnashing teeth. Some gurgling words while others swollen up their necks like actual bullfrogs.

Her breath quickened at the sight of these things. Left hand tensing up on the lantern's handle, despite the sharp pain in her arm.

"Raise the lamp, de'ah. I..."

A forceful gust of wind cut off the spirit as it spoke. A mixture of air and disembodied voices muttering strange words. Clumps of Aes's hair flew forward over her shoulders as it blew past. The mites lost poise. Some fell back onto their hunched backs. They screamed and cried, waving their arms frantically to get away. Each shouting a slightly discernible word. "Yee-ga! Yee-ga!!"

"Whoa, that was scary..." She said with a nervous chuckle.

"...That what'nt me de'ah." The spirit answered. "We are not alone! RUN!"

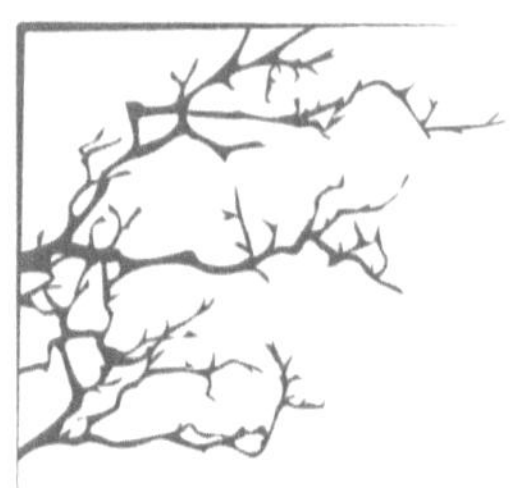

Chapter Four

Aes turned back, staring into the darkness. A deathly chill blew across her face. Catching herself in a stumble, she rushed away despite the wet earth grabbing her shoes. Lantern held high in her right hand, looking left and right for any possible escape, fighting the urge to look back.

"Ov'a the'ah! Stairs!" The lantern spoke.

"I don't see..." She replied.

"On ya, Dex'ta!"

"My what!?"

"THIS HAND CHILDE! THIS HAND!"

"Oh..."

The fluorescent glow showed a symmetric archway, not too far away. Aes waded through the deepening water towards it. Slick moss and glowing mold grew around a masterfully carved stonework. Sturdy, solid, despite the water-worn surface. She slipped occasionally. Mud from her shoes acted as a resin to sustain her balance.

The path elevated to a cooler, drier hallway. Invaded by the natural expansion of root, weed, and brush. Evading, ducking, and vaulting around the thick growth, Aes charged forward. She chanced upon a dead end. The sinking in the pit of her growling stomach lasted only a moment. Hope, illuminated by the lantern, reflects from a small cracked opening in the wall. Maybe large enough for her to squeeze through.

She knelt down, slipping the enchanted light inside first. Was it safer? Was there even time to ponder? Thoughtlessly, in a prone position, shoulders hunched, she slipped both arms in. Shimmying and arching to slip in her upper torso, there came a sudden halt in her struggle.

"My Hips!" she squeaked

"Is this cardinal to our escape?" The Spirit asked with exasperation.

"They are too big! I'm stuck in the hole!" She said again, pushing against the wall.

"Detrimental then?"

"Will you STOP with the big words?!"

"I ascertained Golconda..."

"I need help!" Aes began rocking her hips to help slide through

"A moment. I'll fetch my tools."

"Screw you!" She roared.

"Quiet! You're too loud!" The spirit replied, retaining its calmer tone.

Minutes passed. Aes's unrelenting effort, and slight tearing of her jeans, forced her way out to the other side. A slight gap between the stone wall and a large woven tapestry of decayed linen. Aes slipped from underneath. Light held up to investigate this new location. It didn't have the same degree of glowing fungus as the cave. A mixture of consuming plant life and dusty light from stained windows lights the structure just enough.

From what the original craftsmen had built was ornate, intelligent, and masterful. As if walking into the ruins of an ancient castle. Looking back and forth to discern its purpose proved difficult for Aes. It was too overgrown, but still pleasant.

"This is a bit of an improvement..." Aes stated with a degree of cheer

"Hush... I hear something." The Spirit informed her.

"What?" she whispered.

"Shh..."

She could scarcely hear sounds of rummaging from beyond the doorways. Two of them were on adjacent ends of the room. Cautiously creeping as close to the wall as she could get, Aes advanced towards the quieter of the two.

"Stop!" The Spirit ordered. "Hide!"

"What is it?" Aes whispered back, ducking behind the small trees that spiraled up towards the ceiling. The ambient glow revealed the form of the creature. An enormous nose and bulging eyes were the only discernible features. The rest was a twisted mess of matted hair.

"Goblin. Harmless really." The Spirit told her.

Aes blocked the light from the lantern, staring. The creature limped over to where Aes had entered from. The large linen tapestry painted the image of some form of battle or victory. Looking out over the wall into the distance, it didn't notice her watching mere feet away.

The creature let out a low groan. The goblin scaled the tapestry to the top, pulling at the rings that held it up.

"We have time. Goblins like ta smell everything. They find."

Aes crept through the brush, more stable than the cave. She maintained her balance with more ease. Each step was less of a strain upon her sire legs. She eyed the hairy being like a hawk. Its acrobatic prowess brought it over the top of the linen, plucking the bronze rings one at a time. After it thoroughly sniffed each. Aes shook her head with a sneer at the weird behavior.

She was mere feet away before a break in her concentration.

"STOP!" the spirit ordered in a hush.

"WHAT?" Aes hushed back

"Don't...move! Behind you..." Aes turned her head as slowly as she could.

The door slowly creaked open. A second goblin stepped through. It muttered in an odd language towards the other. It hadn't even noticed the young human kneeling down in front of it. Aes placed her sleeve over her mouth. A ghastly expression on her face from the putrid smell of this creature. The two spoke for a moment as she pushed her back against the wall next to the doorway.

The second goblin hopped upon the limbs of the trees like a squirrel to aid the first. Both sniffing the linen and rings as they pillaged. Aes ducked into the next room, gasping for fresh air.

"Does anything bathe around here?!" she grumbled. There was no reply from the spirit.

This room appeared to be a pantry of some sort. Long wooden open cabinets and tables stood, mostly undisturbed, though it was now picked clean by goblins, most likely. There seemed to be nothing that remained. This realization brought out another loud gurgle from the human's stomach. She sighed and groaned, beginning to scavenge herself.

Through her search, something stood out. A lone small statue, carved into the side of the wall. The figure was feminine. A cloak woven into the stone, shrouding the figure's features. Each arm held a small vase extended out to each side. Aes ran her fingers over the piece. A warm expression on her face. It may have been one of the most beautiful things she had seen in this nightmare.

"This is pretty!" She smiled.

"I've seen one of these before..." The Spirit replied.

Distant muttering broke their contemplation. Aes looked back at the door. The goblins were making enough racket to alert her from a death sleep. As their features came into view. Aes dove under one of the wooden racks. Hiding the lantern within her jacket. She watched their long feet and thin legs walk across the dusty stone floor. Frowning at the waft of their horrid stench. They muttered incoherently near the statue.

Aes peeked up at the two. A thought crossed her mind. How they reminded her of muppets. With their enormous eyes popping from hairy faces. Stick-thin arms with large, long-fingered hands gripped the statue. Struggling to lift it. They seemed to debate the method of which to pilfer the carving. Changing methods multiple times. The young human covered her mouth, snickering as the goblins strained, slipped, bumped heads, and a few times hindered each other in the task.

White air steamed through her fingers. Each breath betrayed the subtle drop in temperature within the room. She had only noticed once the goblins, gasping in exhaustion, huffed at the expense of energy. Neither seemed to notice, at least not right away.

"It's He'ah!" The spirit whispered.

Through the stone archway. Aes watched a compressing gust of white air roll through the cracked hole she had gotten stuck in. Aes caressed the crucifix between her fingers as a presence of unease spilled over into the adjacent rooms. Now the goblins noticed. Ceasing their work, the duo initiated an investigation. The cold mist mimicked a humanoid form. A clawed hand pulled over the ground, the mist following its direction.

Both goblins became visibly disturbed. Backing away slowly, they crept to a second door within the room. Aes watched them both.

"Foll'ah them. They may know the way out!" The spirit instructed.

Aes nodded. Waiting a moment before she moved, attention bouncing back between the growing mist and sneaking goblins. Each step was quiet, save for one careless slip. With the lack of light, Aes couldn't see the uneven, protruding edge of the floor. A soft kick with her shoe, Aes fell to her hands and knees. The lantern slipped from behind her jacket. Clanked loudly as it struck the ground.

The goblins didn't bother to turn back. Hardened pads of their feet struck the ground as they squirmed to get away. The spirit barely got a word out before Aes had snatched the lantern back up and given chase as well as she could, unmatched against their superior agility. Jumping like rabbits. Climbing like monkeys, Aes barely had a chance.

It wasn't them she needed, however, but the path they left. Twigs snapped, dust kicked up, swaying limbs from the intruding plants. Gave her the clue she needed. Aes pushed her sore body once more to survive this eldritch event. The cascading mist stretched through the ruins. Freezing all within its path.

Aes's breath became drier and more difficult. Moving from room to room. Slipping under and between the recent growth. The deathly chill nipped at her heels. She lost the path. Ice built upon the threads of her shoes. She had only taken a moment to discern the route was no longer needed. Quickly, she ran to a vacant opening within the wall. Large enough for her escape. Aes leaped, blindly, though. Striking the outside with a hard thud.

Outside the ruins, a vast forest shrouded the land. Dim radiant beams penetrated the canopy overhead to illuminate the ground. The only sound was that from the goblins. Loading all they could.

"The'ah! The goblins are driving' off in their wagon." The spirit told her.

Aes spotted the two raiders. They weren't alone. Several other goblins pulled a rickety wagon. Cloth tarps held down by nets and worn ropes covered filled sacks of objects. Their strength was slightly surprising. Though after seeing how they moved. Aes understood how such creatures could carry such a load. She scuttled behind them, hopping into the back unhampered.

Wedging herself within, Aes plopped back upon the sacks, kicking off her soaked shoes and socks. Chest decompressing with a releasing of a deep breath. A spacey stare at the linen cloth overhead. She asked again.

"So are you going to tell me who you are now?"

"Call me...Gloam." It finally answered.

"Okay... I didn't think you were going to."

"We have time now."

"Where am I? How did I get here? What is all this? How do I get back home!?"

"Calm yourself, childe, no need to get excited. We are within the Hedge. How? I am not sure. As for getting back? That is why I am here."

"You're going to help me get back home?!"

"Why, of course! Once I can get free from this prison, which I need your help...I will help you get home."

"Oh bet!"

"On what?"

"What?"

"What is this to wager?"

"No, I said 'Bet.'"

"Yes...on what?"

"...never mind." I'll help you!"

"Indeed! Now, rest. You earned it."

With barely a reply. Aes leaned back and drifted off to sleep. Gloam, the spirit, smiled broadly. A twisted, toothy smile and a low chuckle.

A low, howling wind blew. Tall, thin pine trees swayed gently in the breeze. Pale clouds drifted across the sky. The wagon rolled down an unworn path. A strong burst of cold air rushed past them, rocking the wagon. Aes briefly woke, teeth chattering rapidly. She glanced lazily into the forest. She hid herself deeper into the wagon. After noticing several pairs of eyes watching her from within the forest's darkness.

Shivering from cold, and maybe fear as well, Aes sought solace in the closest thing familiar to her world. Leaning her head down, hands clasped together between her rosary.

She whispered several prayers.

"Forgive my long absence... I need your strength. Now, more than ever." She whispered, placing a kiss on the crucifix with a tear in her eye.

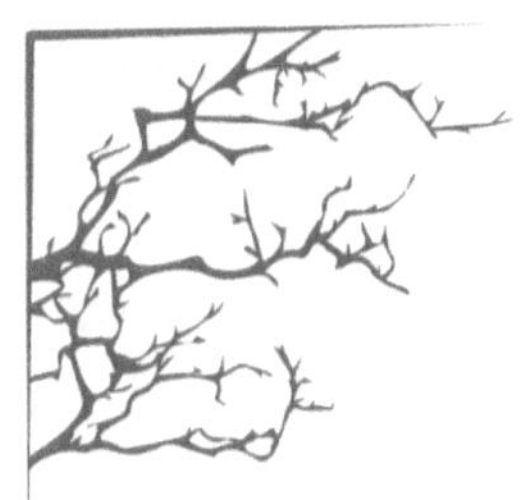

Chapter Five

Aes stared into the darkness of the night. A tight grip on her rosaries. Her face seemed pale, with dark circles around her tired eyes. Something on the pathway caused the wagon to jump. Aes shifted to catch herself. A jolt of pain from her shoulder snapped her out of the trance. A whiff of odor assaulted her nostrils. It was her this time, or rather her damp clothes. Aes began to peel them off.

"Saved up for months, now they are ruined!" She grumbled. Unbuckling the fair pair of leather shoes. Though the air was frigid, it was a welcome for her skin to breathe. Pulling off her leather jacket, she paused for a moment, looking over at the lantern.

"Gloam?" She whispered, hoping for no response. She had no desire to expose herself to a spirit or whatever he was. Gloam gave no response. His light was a soft purple. She whispered to him once more. Again, he didn't respond. She removed her jacket, a yellow shirt underneath, continuing with her jeans and other garments. Draping them over the back of the wagon to hopefully dry.

Aes adjusted herself cautiously, trying to examine her shoulder. It pulsed with a burning sting. Merely tightening her grip sent a shock up her arm. She ran her fingers close to it with gentle ease. She couldn't see it well enough, but maybe her tactile sense could help. It was painful to the touch. The thorn had broken off deep within her shoulder. nearly even with her skin. It would be difficult to remove without a tool.

A strange sound echoed from the woods. Aes turned to look. It wasn't like anything else. It sounded like a mimic of her own voice, crying out in pain. She waited to hear it a second time, but there was nothing. She yawned, rubbing her tired eyes. Maybe it was just fatigue.

She bundled herself up within a linen cloth the goblins had taken. It wasn't much, but enough to keep her covered. Lying against the woven sacks, she closed her eyes. Rosary held tight in her palms.

A heavy dark fog seeped through the brush and foliage. Moving with a motivated purpose. Trailing behind the wagon, it reached up in the form of a hand. Tearing the leather jacket down from the wagon. It ripped and clawed at the garment. Focusing heavily on the left shoulder, where Aes had been injured.

It continued stalking the wagon, taking her yellow bloodstained shirt next. Caressing and squeezing the bloody sleeve. The fog became thicker, blacker, and more solid. It oozed over the cloth until the shirt had been wiped clean from the red stains.

One by one, everything she wore had been seized. Every cut, scratch, and wound soiled her clothes with her own blood. Now there was only one thing left. A single pulp source that called out to this thing.

Aes looked up. Hovering mere yards away, a black shadow trailed after the cart. Its feature is indiscernible and vaguely humanoid. Aes had become as pale as a ghost, stricken with fear as the black form grew in length. Its presumed head dove straight down upon her wounded shoulder, with a stabbing pain so bitter, deathly cold. It froze her from within.

There was a bitter chill. The soft rustling of the trees blowing in the wind. The old carriage being pulled by the goblins, bare feet pushed against moss, muck, rock, and leaves. A distant flickering light from touches pushed away the cold. A wooden gate built from logs that protruded sharp points out at an angle. Threatening anyone brave enough to charge over.

The goblins charged down the path at ungodly speed. Up, around, and the rolling hills. They yipped and shouted as they ran. Sounds of panic and fear.

"Aes, awaken!" Gloam whispered urgently. In a panicked gasp, Aes awoke. Fighting fiercely against the air. Linen cloth fell from her body. The sacks around her were being tossed back and forth.

"Hold on, de'ah. We're bein' chased!" Gloam commanded

"By what?!" She shouted back.

"THAT!" He responded. A black form blocked out any degree of moonlight. A screaming echo filled the sky. Forceful, thunderous winds slammed down upon the pathway, knocking the wagon off balance. The goblins struggled to keep control of the wagon.

"Hold on! We just need to get ov'ah the bridge!" Gloam said. Aes watched as the thing flew through the forest. Its faint outline soared along the branches, severing limbs with sheer force. It arced high into the air, swerving around to make another pass.

Aes watched as the giant thing dive-bombed towards them. The bridge was mere minutes away. She could see the outline of the stones reflecting the firelight. The goblins had landed a single foot upon the waved stone road just as the thing zoomed directly overhead. Aes rushed to the opposite side to see the thing. Moonlight reflected off its feathers, some kind of colossal bird.

She didn't even have time to speak. The aftershock erupted under the wagon, shoving it upon a single wheel. Aes pushed herself against the base of the wagon. Staring down into the abyss with wide eyes. Woven baskets, cloth sacks, and wooden barrels all began to tumble and fall out. A bright glow from Gloam's lantern flew into the air. Aes watched as her companion fell into the darkness, and with a final slam, she joined him.

Her screams reverberated in the night. Arms flailing as she flipped through the air. Images of the bridge's shrinking light faded as she fell into the darkness. A heaviness slammed against her legs. All light and sound became muffled. Her body was enveloped in a feeling of bitter cold as she landed in the rushing water below.

===============================

Along the worn path. Between the deep ruts left by the wagon. A torn pair of jeans, Aes's jeans, rested in front of a tall cloaked figure. Carelessly, this person walked over the trail of scattered clothing. A slight limp with every other step, it held its balance with a sanded stick, decorated with dark feathers and small bones.

Its skeletal, bare feet left no prints as it moved towards a small, hook-shaped object that rested in the ground. Two pricks of green light shone from sunken eye sockets, fixated on what it had found. A bloody briar thorn that had been ripped from Aes's shoulder. Its emaciated arm reached for the thorn. Studying it curiously.

==

Aes broke through the surface, coughing and spitting up water from her lungs. Dark hair masking her face and vision. White light reflected from the water's surface from the scarce beams from the moon. Broken by the ripples and splashes she was making. The water was forceful but not rapid. A constant push that didn't shove her under.

"Gloam?" She called out. Wiping the hair from her face, she searched for the glow from the lantern, but he was nowhere to be found. A burst of wind struck down over the water as the black form of the giant bird flew overhead. Aes slipped lower into the water, watching the creature soar by, kicking her legs to keep her near the surface.

"Gloam?" She called out again. The flow of the water gradually died down. Aes felt soil under her feet, enough to move towards an exit. Though the flowing water was warmer than the air. She swam towards the possible edge. A spark of joy came across her face. She noticed the familiar glow and voice of Gloam.

"Ov'ah he'ah my de'ah" He responded. The lantern rested on a low point in the water. Its glow refracted like several small gems under the water. She quickly swam over to him, her feet still hitting the ground as she pushed forward. She lifted the lantern up out of the water.

"I can't believe we survived that! How is this place so dangerous?" She asked, kneeling down in the water as she spoke to Gloam.

"This ain't nothin' Childe. Of course, it will be much more dangerous if we don't find a road again soon. It is unfortunate. We were so close to that bridge."

"Why is the bridge so important?"

"Beyond that is one of the hollows."

"Okay?"

"The goblins travel through the hedge to trade with the denizens of the hollows." He replied with exasperation. "In any case, several of the goblin's spoils ended up he'ah. I suggest you find somethin' to make yourself presentable."

"Good idea! Uh... don't look, okay?"

"Of course not..." He sighed.

Lifting the light, Aes pulled the sacks and barrels from the water. Searching the contents for something to wear, hopefully ones that were not soaked. She fished through several sacks, spotting several things she could possibly wear. Most were towels, napkins, or visibly too large. There were all sorts of odds and ends. Clothes, trinkets, random useless things.

"Why is it always so dark here?" She asked as she searched. Her eyes lit up as she spotted the rim of a collar. A shirt maybe? It didn't matter. It was something! Immediately pulling it from the sack.

"Dark?" He asked

"Yeah, like it's been night time more than day time. I think it has been like, two hours a day, and the rest has just been dark." Setting the lantern down to rest.

"You have been resting quite a bit."

"Yeah, I guess that makes sense..." She replied, tugging the new clothes down. The tunic she wore came down as far as the sleeves, which draped past her hands. A bit big, it could have been worn by someone taller and more broad-shouldered, but it did the trick. The bottom hem had a slight tear on the left. Slightly darkened from the dirt. Its collar had a string that could tighten or loosen to the middle of the chest.

"I guess this works. I wonder what else they took." She continued to dig through the cargo.

===============================

Through the giant trees, beyond the dense fog and warped vines. A two-story lodge rested quietly in the shadows of the hedge. It was illuminated with deep red lights that swung inside multiple lanterns. Warmly glowing from within, swirls of smoke billow from a robust stone chimney. Well-trimmed evergreens, cypress, and hollies grew within gardens outside. A wooden sign rocked in the blowing winds. A worn medieval design of a horned and hoofed man, pouring a drink into his mouth while holding another in his off-hand. The words 'Tipsy Incubus Pup' etched into the plaque.

The goblins powered their way, full speed, within the picketed gate. The large door opened. A tall, rabbit-like creature and a colorful, bubbly-eyed gnome stepped outside to greet them. The goblins unloaded their wares without instruction and brought them inside. Setting up simple displays for those inside.

Within the lodge. A rather obese female sat lethargically on a well-crafted wooden chair, staring idly at a personal fireplace. A slow drag of her pipe. A tall yellow braided bun rested slightly off center upon her head. Radiant golden eyes, a ball-shaped nose, and large red lips on a plushy face decorated with heavy makeup. Her skin was like bleached ash. A thick white pelt covered her large body. Pulling a pin from a metal brooch, she pricked her thumb and pressed the bleeding digit on a rust-colored wooden statuette of a female figure.

A soft knock at the door of her private quarters She gave a verbal cue to enter. A second female, similar but more stout and dwarf-like in her physique, entered.

"Forgive me intrusion, Head Mistress. The goblins are here...." She began

"Indeed, darling. I'm quite certain the Black-Hearts will be soon as well." She interrupted.

"Aye, Byrne be asking for a shave this time.

"Offer them the usual and see if you can slip in a bit more. You know how those fools expect a discount on top of their 'protection.'" She waved her hand, taking another long drag of her pipe.

"I be thinkin' we may be in good fortune this time." The dwarfish woman said. Closing the door and moving closer "Goblins be gettin' a bit tipsy. Talkin' 'bout hearing voices. One of 'em, called 'em self 'Gloam.'" She whispered with a grin.

The headmistress stared at the dwarf with wide eyes. Giving a big smile before taking the rusty statuette into her chubby hand. Giving it a large kiss.

"Praise you, Mara! I never lost faith." She turned back to the dwarf. "Darling, make sure our 'good friends' are well fed and have plenty to drink. I will have to join them in due time." The dwarfish woman bowed, a large grin on her face as she left the room.

"...Called himself 'Gloam.'" She mumbled, taking another long drag.

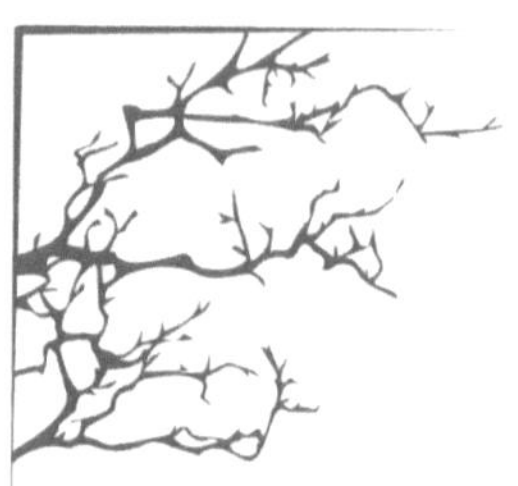

Chapter Six

The clouds swirled in the sky. The trees cracked as they rocked and wrestled. Fell winds moaned as they slipped through stone and wood. A pale mist rolled in like a rogue tidal wave. Mortal screams echoed from the inhabitants of the small towns as they desperately ran in vain. The rolling white buried the land instantly in ice and snow.

With the bitter white mist. Mummified bodies frozen in place. Their faces distorted in expressions of horror and pain. One by one, their heads break free, as if animated by some ungodly force. Looking directly upon a single point. They speak harshly in a guttural language.

"...Coward!"

"...Filth!"

"...Traitor...!"

=================================

The dim purple hue from the lantern rotated through shades of color. Shifting to blue, green, then finally soft yellow as Gloam became more continuous, illuminating the surrounding. Aes was curled up in a pile of woven material she had used for a blanket during the night. Breathing with deep huffs. Her light skin had grown paler, with darkened circles around her eyes. She shivered relentlessly. The sky was a coal ash gray. Dim with rolling clouds and heavy mist. Icy winds whipped around the shoreline, blowing cold water and wet soil towards the two.

"Fin'lay. Good weatha'!" He mocked. "Aes..."

"I'm awake." She responded, "I couldn't sleep at all. My heart kept pounding. I'm so hungry I have a headache."

"Food is not too scarce, but difficult to gath'a, out he'ah."

"I'm so cold..." she whined.

"There is a pelt over the'ah."

"That brown one? It reeks like ass!" Gloam chuckled at her comment.

"You wanna freeze? Mettle is required to survive the hedge." He chuckled, "Now quit ya whin'n. You need to focus on find'n some food and some medicine, ya green'ah than a sprite."

"I checked the baskets and barrels all night, nothing. Just some yellow bottles with roses on them."

"Blue roses? How many?"

"I dunno? A dozen, I think..."

"Blue Rose Orchid is a winery within one of the hollows. Pricey, no doubt they were making a delivery. Find a way to carry it if you can!"

"...You rarely talk, but the moment 'money' is involved, you open up."

"I am merely considering your survival, my sweet childe. Little good wealth can do me, trapped in here."

"How did you get trapped in there?"

"Another time, de'ah..." Aes sighed at his predictable response.

"Why not just leave it here and come back later?"

"If you wish to return to this place." He responded. Shaking her head. Aes worked to gather what was possible. Tying a white cloth around her waist to cover her exposed legs. Packing a few of the bottles into an empty sack. She frowned at the sight of the brown pelt. It was far too cold to go without it. Bitterly, she donned it around her shoulders.

The duo ventured off into the wilderness. Aes could navigate the strange landscape far easier. Though it wasn't much more appealing. The trees towered miles into the sky. Their roots had lifted so far from the ground. It could have been a small village. The young human paced each step forward. As now, she actually spotted the hazards beneath.

The winds grew violent as the two traversed up a small incline. Aes noticed there was hardly any plant life. Nearly everything appeared dead or dormant.

"How can anyone survive out here?" She broke the silence.

"I did... once."

White light barely pierced the overcast, painting the land in an eerie silhouette contrast. As the duo reached the top of the hill, they emerged from the forest to a cliffside overlooking a vast canyon. The air blew colder and harder. Aes almost fell back.

"Where are we going!?" she shouted, trying to be heard over the howling winds.

"Keep ya eyes out for any plant life. Strong herb grows at the end of Lughnasadh." Aes blinked and shrugged at what he said. "Ov'ah The'ah! Gah'lic!"

"What?!" She shouted again.

"Gah 'lic." He replied.

"I'll be straight with you, Gloam. It's really difficult to understand anything you say." She told him, fighting the strong winds.

"I'll assist with that. Ya gonna need to learn the language of the denizens he'ah."

"I really just want to get home. I don't plan to stay longer than I need to." She responded, plucking the roots of garlic from the cliffside.

"Your journey will be much easier if you do. Now, chew the stems and bulb."

"Chew raw garlic?!" She asked, hesitant to follow his instructions.

"Childe... Yes. Chew it until it's mixed with ya saliva." Aes gagged, with a sour face, from the enzymes burning her mouth. "There ya go. Tear off some of that dress ya got, now anoth'ah. Good, spit into the cloth and apply it to ya wound." Aes panted in the cold air to cool her mouth. Gloam chuckled a bit. "Now take that second one and wrap it around to hold the wad in place. That's it! Well done, my de'ah"

Aes kneeled a bit as the poultice juice seeped into her wound. Tears of pain rolled down from her red, swollen eyes. "Now what?" She asked.

"Several. First, survey ya surround'ins. See what ya can find. Aes looked out over the canyon, then back to the forest.

"It all looks the same to me. Lots and lots of nature." She sighed.

"It is the Wyld ya lookin' at, and before ya ask, the hedge is part of the Wyld. Now look to ya sinist'ah, ya wounded side, that is!" Aes turned to her left.

"What am I looking at?"

"Heavy vines grow upon that old stone structure. Ya see it?"

"I think so? All that dark purple?"

"Indeed. That will be our destination for the time. Now, gath'a ya strength. We shall be departin' before that storm rolls in."

"What storm?

"Once ya get familiar with the Hedge and her temperament, y'all learn the signs."

Aes rested for a time. The brown pelt had lost its foul odor from the howling winds that blew from beyond the cliff. Slowly she trudged on. Her bare feet took on reddish blue from the harshness of the temperature. She stopped occasionally to rest and warm herself. Gloam made no objection.

Aes looked out into the horizon of the canyon. Jagged gray rocks held a basin of dark waters. She could clearly see to the other side, a far distance. There was an alien beauty in this place. During each of her pauses, she stopped to admire it just a bit. When she wasn't shivering from the cold,

A soft rumble in the distance rolled up the cliffside and bounced off the trees. The sound of thunder. Gloam was right. A storm was rolling in. Aes hurried to her destination, having no desire to be caught in a freezing rainstorm. It had taken some time, several rests, before Aes had found a sloping path that led towards the building.

A dark cloud smoldered up ahead. Aes caught a glimpse of something less natural, manmade, hanging in the air. A flag, with a sword impaling a black heart over a red field. She reasoned that someone must be there. Fighting through thick brush and foliage. She hopped delicately on her bare toes through the woods, slipping between bush and branch. Slipping down a moss-covered log to more solid ground, filled with quilled pine leaves that forced her to prance over.

"Stop!" Gloam whispered. "Pox upon the Weave! Knolls! You'll have to be cautious going forth, De'ah."

Aes peered through the brush to get a better look. She scarcely spotted a hulking creature. Though it was too far to make out details, it bore a resemblance to a wolf-man. Small yellow eyes and feral features. Clad in some type of paramilitary regalia, arms, and armor, with a surcoat similar to the same black heart and sword image as the flag.

"What should we do?" Aes asked.

"It is too late to turn back. Ya gonna have ta keep ya wits about ya." Gloam replied. Aes looked back towards the tower. Uncertain of how to approach, slipped down under a mossy log, hidden under vines and other small brush. She crawled deeper until fully covered by the leaves and limbs. A crack of thunder and lightning broke the uneasy stillness. Several screams rang out from the woods all around her.

"What was that?" She whispered.

"The reason I tell you to make less noise." Gloam replied.

A long silence passed, and Aes grew more skeptical. What was this? She looked at the small lantern as if to speak. A small creature with glowing red eyes screeched from the limbs above. Aes noticed that its nose seemed to have been cut off, resembling the goblins she had seen before. Its lips were so thin it was difficult to tell if it had gone away. Only jagged rows of shark-like teeth. Something dark brown or rust-colored matted its hair.

The red-eyed monkey screamed so loud. Aes had to cover her ears. Sounds of furious rustling reverberated off the trees. Clawing, scratching, and feral noises came from all around her. Debris from above fell. Leaves, pine, bark, and twigs rained down. Swarms of these red-eyed primates appeared within the trees.

"They emerge when darkness rises. Find a way into the tower before it is too late!" Gloam ordered. Aes took one last listen before emerging herself out from the other side. She tiptoed over the wet ground towards the black heart flag. Maybe there was a path she could find. Looking back several times as she descended a damp slope into marshy puddles.

Her attention split between the wild primates high above and the wolf-like knoll that guarded the tower. She cursed under her breath as two more gnolls appeared at the entrance to the stone structure. The glowing eyes seemed to follow her movement under branches and foliage. Though they did not descend onto the ground. These creatures leap from branch to branch, still staring down in her direction.

Using the distraction, Aes kept a distance as she circled, through the brush, around the ruined tower. Her bare feet were ankle-deep in the cold puddles. There was an ambient glow from an opening to the side of the building, very low to the structure. She looked up several times while moving towards the small hole.

A steady flow of water flowed out from the opening. Taking several deep breaths, Aes steeled herself to enter. Pulling her pelt and skirt up, crouching through the waterway. It elevated to a small grid drain. Covered in leaves and other objects. She peered through the holes to get a better look at the interior, but her view was limited.

Light from the lantern guiding her, she took the angled ninety to her right. She was fortunate. leading to a partly collapsed room. Placing her sack of supplies and the lantern inside, Aes climbed up inside the stone tower's darkened room. Overhead, an old wooden ceiling with several holes with a cascade of vines and thorns, and just beyond, was an old wooden ladder. Just past the forest of thorns.

Leaving the bottles behind. Aes hopped delicately through the thorns and vines. Enduring stabs and cuts. Pulling herself up to the second floor. Aes fell back upon the ground. She finally, to some degree, had shelter from the malevolent elements. At that moment, the storm broke. Hard rain pelted the worn stones. Flashes of lightning illuminated the sky. Earth-shattering thunder rocked the very stones, though the fact that they still stood was a testament to their construction.

Aes tightened the pelt around her, warming her wet feet. With a deep sigh, she closed her eyes for a brief rest. There was, however, a fine smell that tickled her nose, triggering a sharp pain in her stomach. The smell of roasting meat. Through the small cracks in the wall, she spotted an enormous bird, plucked clean. Hanging over a smoldering flame, its blackened skin dripped with meaty juice into the hissing fire. Aes started with the look of a feral animal. She had not eaten in maybe three days.

It didn't matter. If she missed this chance to eat, she might not get another, and she would most certainly die.

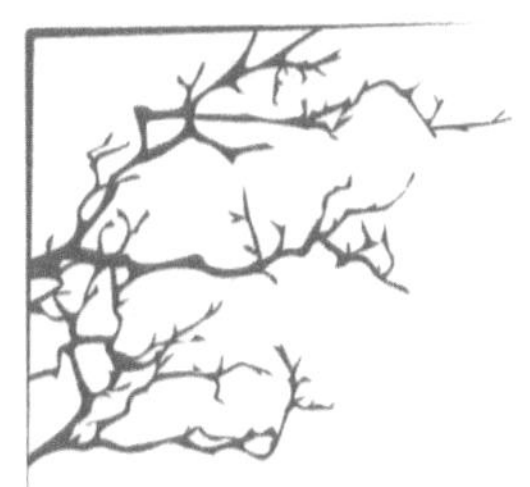

Chapter Seven

A gentle tapping of wood to stone reverberated down the canyon. Its meditative rhythm eased the rampant behavior of the wildling. Their red eyes peered from the trees down to the cloaked figure that strolled along the cliffside, caressing a large briar thorn within its bony fingers. Fearful, the wildlings were eerily silent, not a movement among them.

The rain drizzled down, tapping upon the heavy cloak of the gault wanderer. Unfazed by the change in atmosphere and weather. The cloaked wanderer stared down, over the edge, upon the ruined tower below, raising the thorn up, aiming it slowly back and forth, like some kind of compass. The motion stopped once the thorn aimed down upon the ruins of the tower.

Its skin twisted as the wanderer grinned on one side of its face. With a rise of its staff, the wildlings leaned out from the trees, their long, thin limbs tensed, staring at the wanderer in wait.

==

Aes leaned in towards the floor, peeking through the worn stones and wooden beams. The three wolf-like gnolls stood on guard towards the open entrance, crude weapons in their robust, clawed hands, spotting an opening to squeeze through. Thick vines clung to the walls beyond the opening. Slipping her hand through, Aes tugged hard several times on the vines. They seemed secure. She slowly removed her pelt and extra attire.

Gloam was quiet as Aes slipped through the opening, feet first. Her injured shoulder made the descent more difficult, with her weakened grip, but the vine was thick enough for her to place her feet over it.

She looked back several times to watch the knolls. They seemed more concerned with something in the forest.

One after the other, her feet eased upon the cold stone floor. Tugging the loose tunic back up to cover her shoulder, she crept low towards the smoky flame, staring with large eyes at the roasted bird, nearly 3 feet long, charred black, still drizzling with melted fat. She didn't hesitate to grab the carving utensils and hack off pieces to eat. She winced at the hot, greasy meat burning her fingers but gulped it down shortly after. It was moist and fresh. She licked the juice from her fingers, preparing for the next piece.

A few times she looked beyond the spit to watch the knolls. A low growl from the corner stole her attention. It was a massive black-furred hound that bared its sharp teeth at her. It moved forward like a stalking tiger. Aes raised the cutting tool at the beast. It barely moved forward with a loud bark before the chained collar on its neck caught the beast mid-leap. It made far too much racket.

Aes didn't even look past the spit to watch the knolls. Rushing back to climb the vines and slip back through the opening. The beast barked and jumped, the chain around its neck choking it with each charge. One of them approached the large animal. With a roar of his own, the gnoll struck the beast hard in the snout. The animal cowered, still watching Aes climb the vines.

She had one knee placed through. Her escape halted instantly as something seized her by the ankle with a crushing grip. Aes was yanked back out by the large wolf-man, leaving her held high in his grasp. With burning eyes, he stared at the human, who was maybe around half his size, holding her up by the scruff of her tunic. He called out to the others.

The three wasted no time. Lifting a grid from the floor, they tossed the young woman down into a reservoir drain, creating a loud splash as she fell upon her hands and knees within. The steady stream of icy water, flowing in from the rain, rose midway to her calves. Aes stood, glaring up at the mocking faces.

"Let me out!" She demanded, her petite hand grabbing the grid, trying to push up on it. All three grinned and snarled in response. One chewed on the leg of a large bird, mouth open, in front of her. Pieces of food fell from its open mouth. Her chipped nails dug into her whitening palm. With gritting teeth and tearful, glaring eyes, she roared up at them.

"STOP LAUGHING AT ME!!" Her scream reverberated off the stones of the ruins, echoing out into the darkness of the forest.

Aes hid from the sight of the knolls and their hyena laughter, satisfied with their sport. The water increased in flow as the storm came down harder. She sat upon a small stone elevation built into the structure, breathing deeply as she fumed with rage. Muttering curses and insults about the savage wolf-men. Shivering almost uncontrollably from the cold.

==================================

A flash of lightning illuminated the still form of the cloaked wanderer, breaking through the night. Bringing down the staff upon the cliffside rock. The wildlings screeched, either from fear or excitement, fleeing from their haven in the tree, descending upon the canyon below.

One knoll turned his attention outward towards the trees. A feral sneer on his sour face, yellow eyes glaring into the shadows. He snorted as he saw the swarm of red eyes raining down upon the tower with ear-shattering sounds. Rising with his savage weapon, he let out a lion's roar. Spittle and meat spewed from his maw. The other two joined him against the wildlings.

Within her prison, Aes heard Gloam speak through the shadows. "De'ah?"

"I'm h-here," she huffed, struggling to stay alert. "Wait..." Aes noticed something. As the water flowed in, it didn't rise, despite the flooding waters from the storm. "This is go-ing somewhere." She braved the frigid waters to inspect the smooth stones. "It's just big e...nough." She hesitated, looking back up to the grind. She knew it may be her only way out.

"'Tis a reservoir, I believe," Gloam whispered through the shadows. The waters came up just below her knees. Aes reached into the aqueduct's structure. "It will be difficult, Childe. Keep ya mind focused, no, not f'ah."

"Yeah, okay, wait... How can you s-see me?" Aes asked, looking around.

"Ne'vah mind that now. Focus!" He ordered. Aes huffed, taking in several deep breaths to psych herself. Taking one last inhale before submerging her head under the waters.

The shock of the cold hit her hard, gradually impeding her mental focus. Aes reached out with both hands, one to feel the way. The other to pull herself, which took little effort from the water pushing her forward. Her fingers ran over the fine sandy stones. Her feet got lightly scratched from kneeling too close. The cold water gripped down on her shaking body, her muscles losing coordination as her movement became less controlled. She teetered on the edge of consciousness.

"Ya almost out de'ah." Gloam whispered. "...De'ah? Aes?" There was no response. The cold waters flushed from the tower's stone drain. Aes, now a soft purple in hue with no responsive movement, along with it. "Aes!" Gloamed called out again. Still there was no response.

===================================

Heavy rains drenched the three knolls, each fought as ruthlessly as they appeared, like savage barbarians, to ward off the howling beasts. What seemed like two dozen, at least, of these wildling apes bit, grabbed, clawed, pounded, and jumped all over the militiamen. Each of them swung mighty blades hard, cutting through several of the wildlings at a time, slamming them down, stomping, and crushing their little bodies.

More of the wildlings hailed from above, ripping chunks from the exposed flesh of the wolf-men, some retreating from injury or with the fallen back into the woods. One warrior had been targeted the most. He fell to his knee from the intensity of his wounds. Still he fought fiercely. With only a couple of the wildlings left to fight. He aimed his weapon at them definitely. The primal creatures grabbed the dead and even pieces of their destroyed bodies. Fleeing back into the trees,

Perched upon a crumbling stone atop the stone tower. The cloaked figure looked down upon the victorious yet wounded gnolls. One by one, they spotted the figure, its silhouette backing against the flashing skies. The three prepared themselves once more for battle, but as a crack of lightning boomed across the sky, the figure was gone.

With wide eyes and snarling faces, the largest of the three ordered a tactical retreat. The smaller two obeyed without question. They vanished into the forest, leaving many things behind.

==================================

Eerie green flames danced atop pillars of tall black candles, their deathly radiant glow illuminating Aes' unconscious body. She lay out, stretched over a stone table. Occult implements and tools surrounded her body—dark gemstones, bowls of flora, herbs, animal skulls, and a short blade. ooming over her was the cloaked, gaunt figure, studying her shoulder wound.

The bony fingers sifted through jars of powder and poultice. Applying strange ointments to her wounds and other parts of her body, flush life returned to her freckled, lily-white cheeks. Aes breathed deeply in her unconscious state.

Presenting a hooked bone needle, the cloaked figure pricked the young woman's finger, soaking the ivory pin in fresh blood. With delicate and professional precision, ran the needle through the human sound in cross-stitch fashion. Its eldritch properties created a thread that knitted Aes's flesh back together seamlessly. A final ointment was applied over the wound, a faint smell drying out the moisture.

The candles had lost about four to five inches from their wick. Aes gradually came into consciousness, springing up with a startled look. The ungodly glow of the green flames bounced off glass jars sitting on open cabinets and tables. A faint bluish-green mist leaked from the stones underneath, swayed as a shadow moved about from the corner of her vision. Aes snatched a black blade that rested beside her on the cold stone table.

She felt a gentle tug of her hair with something cold. Turning around with the blade raised to face…nothing, nothing that she could see.

Aes searched for a means of escape. There was none. No door or window, just a cocoon of mossy stones that reflected the green candle lights that occasionally dimmed from a darting shade. Aes spun in circles a few times.

"Where are you?" She whispered, her eyes darting from side to side. Something brushed against her head again. A mixture of scream and battle cry escaped her lips as she blindly swung the blade behind her, striking hard a rolled cloth sack suspended from the ceiling. It fell to the ground, the rope having been cut from the blade's edge.

The room began to shift and warp, as if she was seeing double. Aes struggled to keep her balance. A shadowy form walked towards her quietly. Aes turned to face it, but it too was fading from her sight. Everything dimmed until Aes stood alone in the black void. She could see only her own body.

The soft sounds of cracking glass echoed in the vast abyss. Aes turned to see from where, with each movement, the cracking became louder and louder. She looked down, whence the noises were coming, to see her own reflection underneath her. She hoped to get away. The reflection shattered into tiny pieces as Aes fell into nothing.

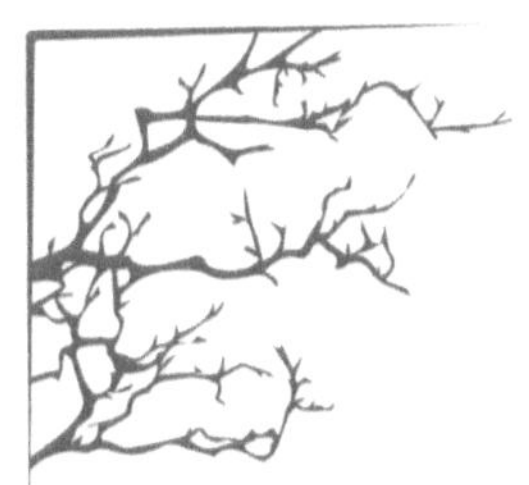

Chapter Eight

Unable to scream, Aes drifted slowly into darkness, as if being sucked down into a watery vacuum, despite being dry. Her hair and tunic fluttered, drifting in gentle ripples over her body. The fall became less surreal and more mortal as she gained speed. A faint image came into view. The blackness of the void dissipated in a haze. She witnessed it all.

A sharp chill shot up her legs. A cold wind stroked her hair over her shoulders. She looked all around. The land was alight and sane once again. The dark forest surrounded her, icy waters stroking her bare thighs. Had she awoken from a strange dream? How much of this was a dream? How much was real?

She stumbled over a slick rock, one that had been used as a dam for the waterway. The blade she had taken fell into the dirt, point first. She tore it from the soil, running her fingers along its edge, jerking her hand back from an accidental cut. Her chest heaved as she fell on the side of her knees, watching the flow of red from her index and middle fingers, shaking her head in confusion.

"Aes!" Gloam called from the darkness. Aes looked back. The tower was not too far. Its dim glow from the dying fire. Weakly, she stood, and with clumsy steps rushed towards its solid structure.

"Gloam!" she answered, weakly.

"The knolls are gone, but be careful." He instructed. Aes carelessly crawled through the first opening into the ruined sanctuary. She ignored the remains of meat over the spit, the foliage poking through the ground, or even the stains of blood. Climbing back through the hole to her companion, Aes brought the enchanted lantern to her chest. Her head turned with unease, rosaries in her trembling left hand, placed against her head as she combed and chewed on her hair with the right, also shaking.

"What is this place…?" She whispered, cradling herself.

"It's the hedge, Childe. It is merciless. Keep ya wits about ya." Gloam whispered, "I can ease ya mind again, but my pow'ah is limited. Speak 'Kyrre.'"

"K-yrre." Aes replied, still struggling to breathe. The soft glow from the lantern filled her eyes once again. Her breath settled as her behavior calmed. Aes pulled the pelt back over herself.

"The'ah might be some more of that roast below." Without a word, Aes climbed back down to the base, sitting herself close to the fire pit. The large bird had been nearly picked clean. There was enough meat that was still warm that she fed herself with. She ate slowly. The glow in her eyes remained as she ate with dignity. "Rest while you can, De'ah. Gnolls gonna be return'n."

The glow gradually faded from her eyes as she nibbled on bits of warm meat. Using a wooden cup, she drank bits of fat and gelatin.

"Why am I here?" She asked idly.

"The hedge has a will of its own. It takes who it wants."

"You say that like this place is alive!"

"I'tis." He confirmed, Aes had a look of fear again. "I figure now is as good a time as any to tell ya. The hedge twists in on itself, kill'n and eat'n anything and everythin'. It continues to grow and grow. Few can survive its pow'ah. That is why we need to gotta git to the nearest hallow, any hallow, at this rate."

"How is that possible?"

"Dunno, could be ancient magic, could be somethin' else. I just know what, not why. Fortunately, you have me to guide you!" He chuckled with a strange grin. "Now don't be ask'n all them questions. You eat and rest ya head. Once this storm passes, we gonna head out. Hopefully before 'em gnolls come back."

"What makes you think they will?"

"Gnolls is the most greedy, envious, flea-ridden waste of spit. They let all this rot, then let anyone else have it." He told her. A flash of lightning lit up the woods outside. Aes bundled herself up tighter in the pelt for a rest. The rhythmic rain tapping against the sounds eased her fears, though she was still too restless. A second flash illuminated a disturbing image.

Aes sat up, startled. The giant body of the black hound she had faced lay in its corner, motionless. Aes lifted the lantern to inspect it, remembering it had been on a chain. The creature was bloodied and still. Red stains ran in trails from the floor to the stone archway. Cautiously, she inspected the creature. Faint huffs of breath came from its nostrils.

"Poor thing..." she whispered. A single eye burst open, pupils shrank in the lantern's light. It lunged at the young human before she could react, its narrow snout baring its teeth and barking viciously. The chain choked down on its neck once more. Any closer, it would have the poor girl in its maw. The force of its powerful body nearly tore the chain from its post.

"What are you doin'?" Gloam shouted

"I was just curious!." she answered, crawling backwards on the floor.

"Child, ya curiosity will be ya undoin'. That leash is 'bout to break. GIT!!" Aes turned around as she stood up. There was no escape beyond the stone archway that led out to the raging storm. She pressed her back against the stone wall. She was barely five feet away from the beast, narrow jaws clamping down at her. She sidestepped carefully to her left, watching the beast strain on its leash, which was gradually loosening the fire pit, the only thing that stood between them.

Several tools that were leaning against the wall fell from their posts. Aes spotted a large shovel. Taking a last look at the beast, she used it to throw chunks of embers and ashes into its eyes. The beast yelped in pain. It yelped as it began clawing itself back to retreat, pawing its snout and snorting several times.

Aes tossed the shovel to the side, grabbing the lantern and blade. She rushed towards the archway, halting just before the opening, the black rumbling clouds and hard flooding rains before her. She shook her head at the sight, but what were her options? Stay in an old ruin and starve? Be ripped apart by a giant hound? Or face the bitter elements of the hedge. No choice was preferable!

"Wish I had some shoes..." Aes muttered, taking several strong inhales and charging into the storm. She winced at the feeling of sharp cold needles plucking at her bare skin.

Perched atop the tower, the cloaked wanderer watched the young human scamper off into the woods. Its glowing green eyes looked back to the cliffside as black, clawing mist flowed down into the tower. The radiant light from the fire dying out, and a violent yelp from the hound echoed throughout the canyon.

==

Within the homely lodge of the Tipsy Incubus Pub. The dwarven women tended to a large boar, slowly roasting over an open spit. Sipping a pint and returning three other empty mugs to a flat-headed ogre behind a dark oak bar. A cold wind slipped through as a knoll opened the door.

"There he be..." The dwarf said. The feral creature gasped at the sight of the gnome standing just before the entrance, a wide, shark-toothed grin, two off-colored eyes, one a dull green, the other a golden yellow. Her white hair braided with purple and pink ribbons, she presented a large pair of shears.

"No! Not you! Stay back!" The gnoll growled. The gnome took several steps towards the wolf-man. A menacing cackle, as she approached. "No, you're not cutting my hair again!!" The gnoll protested.

"Maple! leave 'em be!" The dwarf intervened, flicking droplets of water at the grinning gnome.

"AH! Not the salt! Not the salt!" She squealed as the droplets singed her slightly. waddling away.

"Go clean something, or catch a cricket!." The dwarf said. "Sorry, Byrn, want yer usual...by Mara, what happened to ya?" She asked, staring at his wounds.

"Yeah, usual trim. Might git me a promotion. And, uh, nutin much. Outpost got overrun by hobgoblins."

"Yeah, yeah. Come sit. Ya can tell me all a'boot it." She instructed, leading the Gnoll to a seat in front of a thorn-framed mirror. He followed her, a fearful jump as the gnome clapped the shears at him one last time.

"We was hold'n this spot out in the canyon for a bit, orders, ya know, goin' well as could be expected. The Shuck hound was act'n funny, though. He said, as the dwarf cleaned her tools and placed a cloth around his neck. "Had a good kill from a boobie we found. Figure it settles the nerves. We's been hearin' strange sounds in the woods, hough. Grif thought it might have been hags. He was always a mite spooked since that one time..."

"Heh, right?" The dwarf commented, snipping the knoll's sideburns.

"Right, now get dis. We sees the trees, filled to the brim with red eyes. We all knew it was 'em redcaps."

"Redcap hobgoblins? No wonder ye got such nasty bite marks."

"Mhm. That wasn't the queer thing, though. They was just sittin' there in the trees, starin'. Then the shuck starts barkin'. No sooner had I gone to shut em up. I seen this...thing!"

"What did it look like?"

"Queerest. Couldn't tell if it was an elf or what. She was hidden' in one of em holes in the tower."

"Tower? In the Canyon? How does this look, Good?"

"Erm...Bit more on the sides, blend it real good-like. Yeah, one of em ol' towers. Grif says it belongs to a Pale'n."

"Pale one? The necromancers?"

"I dunno, just what he said. Maybe it was. We see somethin' up on the top. Well, Griff says he did. I didn't sees it."

"So what a'boot that elf thing ya saw?"

"Oh yeah, funny lookin' screamed a lot too. Tossed it in the hole, spoke something I ain't never heard before. Seems like it was talkin' to itself too."

"How queer. You say it be a lass?"

"Aye. Couldn't mistake that for a sec."

"Is she still at the tower? Why would ye want to take it anywho?"

"Aye, ain't no way gitten outta that hole, and eh, Sargent really doesn't want me talk'n 'bout that."

"Com'on, This be Lily ye be talkin' to. Ye know I love me a good bit o juice."

"Hm, yeah, alright then. Sargent says he wants us checkin' every tower we's find. Not sure what for, but we's gotta."

"Ye remember how to get back?"

"Course I do. I'm the best strider in these hollows."

"Indeed, Aright give this a look." She said, stepping away from the mirror.

"Hm... yeah, yeah!" He said, admiring the haircut. The dwarf smiled and nodded. Glancing up towards the wooden balcony overhead. The shadowy outline of the headmistress stood, watching and listening to the entire conversation as she puffed her pipe with a wide grin.

"Well, if that is gonna do ye, get ye a bath and a pint. Ye had a time, it seems." The dwarf said, brushing off the knoll as he stood up. "By the by..." She continued. Byrn turned back to the dwarf. "Would ye lads be interested in makin' some extra shinnies? Headmistress might be havin' a job for ye." She said, gesturing upstairs towards the large female.

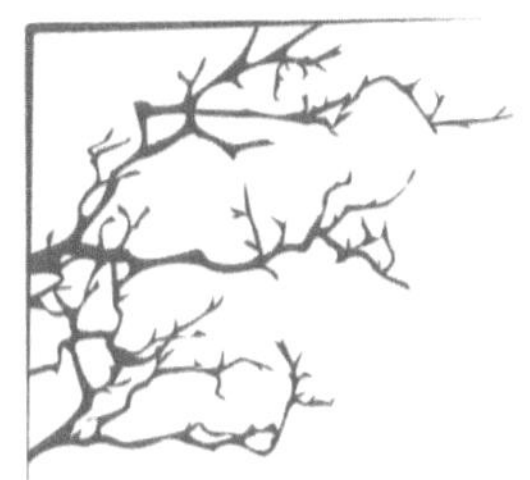

Chapter Nine

The light from the hearth dimmed. Its smoldering flames snuffed out from the freezing black mist that hovered over the stone floor. The black hound lay in the center. Its eyes glossed over, tongue protruding from its mouth. A flash of lightning illuminated the inside of the ruined tower. The twisted shadow of the eldritch haunt leaned over it. An unearthly chorus of voices spoke from the mist.

"Pitiful beast." A clawed hand rose from the mist, inserting black tendrils into the nose, eyes, and mouth of the lifeless hound. "Take my essence!" The hound's body began to budge and twist in unnatural ways. Sounds of ghastly breaths and cracking bones. "Serve me in darkness!" Its body spasmed violently.

"Bring me the blood of the Man Childe!...So that I may LIVE once more!" The hound rose to its feet. Upright posture and fierce snarling. Tiny green flames flashed in its pitch-black eyes. Immediately, it captured the scent and dashed off into the storm!

==============================

The rain continued on, its steady drumming padded over the grotto Aes had discovered. She huffed and groaned as she rubbed a stick over another.

"That's not the way." Gloam said. "Peel the bark from that one, no, no, the oth'ah. Tie it to one end, as if it was a bowstring, now the oth'ah. Bend it back. Good. Now sharpen that oth'ah. Wait..." Aes paused during the instructions. "Where did ya get that blade?"

Aes looked at the strange dagger she had been carrying around. "I don't know, I had this strange dream that..." She paused, pulling the yoke of her tunic down. She exposed her shoulder. Gently rubbing her fingers around the wound. "It's been stitched up..." she murmured.

"Ya had a dream..." He inquired.

"Yeah, and I picked this up and, I don't know. I just woke up with it. Why?" Gloam was quiet, an obvious hesitation to respond.

"It's very 'ornate'..."

"Okay?" Aes asked.

Gloam said nothing further about it. Aes looked at the lantern, wondering what he was hiding from her. "Use it to sharpen the oth'ah stick to a point. Now, twist the string around the stick. Use the point to create friction in the tind'ah." Aes worked diligently to make the fire. Time passed. Her strength waned. Tiny wisps of smoke emerged. She groaned and pleaded for something to catch, but there was nothing.

Aes slammed the sticks down several times in anger, the string partly coming off the bow. "Why is this so hard?! Why is everything I do?" She stood up in a huff, pacing the ground in frustration. Gloam, calm as always, watched her vent for several minutes.

"What makes ya think ya gotta get ever'ah thing right the first time?" Gloam asked.

"Because when I was growing up... just. Never mind!" She moped.

"Failure is part of learn'n. Only way yo gonna survive out he'ah is to learn." He told her. "Also, using some of ya hair may help get it started." Aes looked at the lantern, combing her black curls nervously as the cold winds seeped into the grotto, easing her temper gradually. She looked at the strange dagger, still idly combing her hair with her fingers.

"How much? I don't want it to look uneven."

"Ya appearance is the least of ya worries. Ya need to understand."

She picked up the ornate blade once more, with great hesitation and several pauses. She took a lock of her hair before the blade's edge. Breathing deeply, she clenched her eyes shut and sliced off a handful. The blade fell from her hand onto the ground. She had a grim expression. She placed the curls over the wood and used her crafted tools once more.

The wisps of smoke grew into dim lights that brought a small smile to her face. Though she continued idly combing the section of hair she had cut off.

"Blow gently and build it up. Place small pieces around it. The heat will catch. No! smaller than that!" Gloam instructed. The soft glow from the flame warmed the small area of the grotto. Providing the young human was a haven for respite. Aes moved closer to the small fire, gradually building it with Gloam's instructions.

The two said little to each other. Aes drew into the ground different images and words. Gloam seemed to face the opening of the grotto, his translucent features frowning at something.

"Alex?" He murmured. Aes sat up at the name.

"Alex? What?" She inquired.

"N-Nothing De'ah."

"No," she said, crawling over the lantern. "You said, Alex, what about him!? Is he here?"

"No! I was in thought!" Gloam insisted. She sighed deeply and lay down. "Ya need to rest. We may be here for a while." Aes made no reply. She simply stared at the small fire, whispering the words 'I miss you.' as she closed her tired eyes.

===

"Ya just want the thing we caught?" Bryn asked. Stroking the hairs on his face and chin. The headmistress nodded slowly, smoke from her pipe billowing around her. The Knoll raised an eyebrow. "What for?"

"I suspect this creature has taken something that rightfully belongs to me!" she responded with a grin.

"So it is a 'fief! I knew it! That'll sure take a load off Grif's mind. He aint been right since that one time. He sees hag magics everywhere!"

"So it's settled then? When the goblins go to take your supplies to this outpost of yours, they will bring it back to me?"

"I dunno. Sargent says all 'fiefs get the axe. Personally, I'd say we should cook it! Had some pretty big mutton chops. Those looked tasty..."

His mug was topped off as he pondered, despite the roasted meat, grilled fruits, and warm rolls laid out before him. "Wait, you ain't bribing me, are ya?"

"Byrn, Dah'ling, would 'I' do such a thing?" The headmistress asked coyly.

"I guess not?" he shrugged, before scarfing down the food.

"Indeed, oh, and do make sure to return my precious, uh..." The headmistress shuddered to remember, looking at Lily, who was miming out carrying a lantern. "Lantern, yes! Precious heirloom! Oh, the restless nights!" She feigned, though Byrn was too distracted by his feast. "Byrn?!" The Knoll looked up, a chunk of meat falling from his face. "The lantern as well?" He gave a solemn nod before going back to gorge himself.

The headmistress grinned as she stood up. "Perfect, now please excuse me. I have many letters to write and must get prepared for a VERY special guest." She softly cackled as she left the room.

===

The reanimated hound dug his narrow snout into the brush. Following the human's strange path. She stayed close to the large rocks by the flowing stream, leaving no physical prints, intentionally or unintentionally. Unfazed, the hound continued his hunt. Expanded senses detected a wisp of strongly mixed emotions. Fear. Anger. Confusion. Though the strong winds thinned out the scents, her track was not so easily covered.

He paused for a time. Sharp ears twitched and turned to the sounds of echoing voices, fading in and out. They echoed from the stones and trees. The beast stepped cautiously towards the higher-velocity sounds. They mixed with the human's scent, which had left a trace of strong smells of physical strain.

He howled another otherworldly noise with his newly gifted life energy that sounded like the dissonant voices of lost spirits. The beast was on the hunt. Trailing through the shadows of the dark forest, it leaped over logs with mighty limbs, powered through vines and brush with its broad frame. The heavy chain around its neck flapped in the air behind it, cracking limb and stone like a vile whip.

The echoes of the voices were clearer, and the scent grew stronger. His prey was close. The hound's long jaws opened, bearing large, sharp teeth. With a giant leap, the hound flew into the air. A strong crack of thunder and lightning lit up the sky. The hound landed just at the edge of a small cliff.

A warm glow from the other side nearly blinded the hound. The extension of his senses fortified with the vitality of the phantom. The beast faded back into the shadows, away from the luminous radiance. The scent was overwhelming. He had found his prey resting before a small opening on the cliffside—a simple grotto elevated just over a flooding stream.

The hound perched himself within the shadows of the brush. The green flames from his eyes stared at the single spot. His instincts had been hardened, even beyond life. He watched and waited patiently.

Gloam stared back from his own point across the water. His glowing hue shifted to brighter colors. "Aes," he began. She didn't answer. Looking back to call out to the human once again. She had placed the last of the kindling over the small flames of the hearth and fallen asleep next to it. "Aes!" he called out again. She did not respond.

Gloam looked back out towards the grotto's opening. Vigilantly observing the tree line on the other side. Its erratic yet predictable flow of movement from the winds showed glimpses of something—something watching and waiting in the dark.

==

Sloshing through the murky swamps, a tall, hunchbacked figure looms. Its long arms stabilize its body with a crooked stick. A faint aura of luminescence emanated from multiple lanterns tied to the walking stick. A single bulging, discolored green eye peered from under thin, scraggly hairs and a weathered, woven rag shawl.

The anorexic giant stopped in front of a hallowed tree, reaching its long arm inside. It caressed the remains of a broken rope.

"Seems a prisoner has escaped." A low, inhuman voice spoke from behind. It's four green eyes staring at the empty three.

"That little gutter snipe, I shan't speak ill of his resourcefulness." The one-eyed giant wove the lanterns over the swamp water in a circle. Revealing a dark reflection of the events "The Shadow has been manipulated. But by whom? It is of no consequence. Be his power shall be mine! Mara, take all those who stand before me..."

The giant pulled another small lantern from a belt. Hanging it within the tree's hallowed center.

"Grandmother. Allow me to..." The giant raised its clawed hand to silence the four-eyed beast.

"You and your brother, guard my 'guests.' I shall retrieve Gloam and feast on the bone of this trespasser." The giant croaked, her body mutating into a different creature. Arms and back sprouting quills, her long nose hardening to a beak. She took flight into the darkness of the hedge.

The small lantern she left behind radiated with sporadic shifts in colors of yellow, orange, and red. Within the twisted metal frame, a small figure could be seen, striking its fist on the glass, an expression of panic and despair.

About the Author

https://substack.com/@knightsofautumncrown

Also by Marco Tomasz Duraj

Blood Hunt: Book 2 of Knights of the Autumn Crown Series. The Inquisition of Alejandro. The Goth.

The Goth

Told as a poetic edda by a strange older man. The Goth tells a dark story of a savage North man, cursed by the Norse gods...